HOO

ISSUE SIX:
Positivity

CROWVUS

2024

© Copyright 2024 Crowvus

All works of writing and art © Copyright 2024 retained by contributors.

All rights reserved. This book or any portion thereof may not be reproduced or used in any manner whatsoever without the express written permission of the artist or writer, except for the use of brief quotations in a book review.

All works are the property of the artist/writer. To preserve the authors' unique voice, poetry and prose remain unedited.

Website: www.crowvus.com
Email: the_team@crowvus.com
Twitter: @CrowvusLit

Edited by Crowvus

Cover Illustration by **Nathan Dumlao**

Editor's Note

The world is in a dark place at the moment. It is all too easy to be swallowed up by the negativity of world politics and the lack of humanity. So we decided to make this issue of Hooded all about **Positivity**.

We were initially disappointed by the uptake on this theme, and had to put out a prompting call for more contributions. The result? A fabulous collection of positivity in written form.

We hope you will be uplifted by all the positive vibes and that it will, at least in part, help you keep a little optimism in today's world.

Thank you for sharing in this issue of Hooded.

the Crowvus team

Contents

Editor's Note

The Move

Jane Murton Armer

My Warning

Elizabeth Carey

Cobwebs

Elizabeth Carey

A Cat Called Connie

S. Bee.

Dichotomy

Leigh Sosville

The Luckiest Boy in the World

Steve Wade

Near Catastrophe

Brenda Lawrence

Thanks a Bunch

Brenda Lawrence

Ornithologising

Greg Michaelson

The End of Helen L.'s Dream

Robert Tateson

The Move
Jane Murton Armer

It was snowing when we loaded up the van. My mum and dad loading boxes while I stood watching and bouncing a baby. I remember looking down the street, the red bricked houses hemmed in like sardines on a bus. A red door, a black door, blue, green and white. I'd always hated this street, the only thing we could afford. The street with Mr Shaffi's corner shop that sold the lewd mags on the top shelf and kids hung about in the evening puffing cigarettes in their puffa jackets and eating skittles, swigging Fanta from a plastic bottle.

In the van with all we owned, we left that cold, damp city, a rancid place with all hope squeezed out.

A few months earlier Christine said I was running away; I should be content to live in the burbs as she calls it. It's what people like us do, we leave school, black kitten heels tapping on the lino in the hairdressing salon, discussing your holiday plans whilst setting a perm all for a monthly wage packet. You meet a boy on a Friday night, one night rolls into a few dozen, mum cooks a frozen pizza for tea and you pack your bags for a two bed terraced on Chapel Street.

We settled down, Rich and I, and I settled for a life without aspirations. At six am Rich hits the snooze on his phone, except for weekends and five weeks holiday a year. Up ladders tiling roofs while I sit at home with the baby. Mum puts the washing on so I can put my feet up, again. I eat another packet of cheese and onion and watch A New Place in the Sun, mum peels potatoes for a pie I don't make because I've still got my feet up, third cup in hand.

Mikey died on a late summers evening, the sun shimmered off the blistered tarmac like huge boils bursting. He'd been driving home from Paula's, taken the sharp bend too sharp on Pike Road and skidded like a skittle into a wall. Snapped his neck and died on the way to hospital. We filed into that funeral parlour a hot mess of stinging tears and a future robbed. Paula cried and I had half a shandy in The Queens Head. Kisses flowed and the tears dried. Rich looked at me and I was glad it wasn't him.

That night I said to Rich the hills and sea are calling to me. We've got to do it Rich, shrug off those old disappointments and build a life in a new free place, a life I know I can't find smack bang in the middle of this muddle. That long hard stare of his sparked a hope, and I stared back into those sapphire eyes with a splash of gold. We googled a new life, and Rich went to Lidl's to get cardboard boxes.

It was a Tuesday when Rich's mum came round and cuffed his ear. Accused me of brainwashing him, said I was too hoity toity now I'd left the salon for a proper job and bought a Laura Ashley sofa. She said this was a good a place as any, and we needn't think she was travelling halfway up the country to see the baby. I was tearing the family apart, taking away her only granddaughter.

Rich slammed the back door on the way to work. I phoned my mum who told me those hills and that sea are mine. I told her they're slipping away, Rich's getting cold feet, my hearts a sinking stone. Pull yourself together love, she said, that baby your bouncing on your knee deserves the world. Give her the world. Give her those hills and that sea and watch her fly. She deserves to fly, and so do you.

Rich came home, the door didn't slam. He plucked packing tape from his pocket, and I put the radio on. We filled boxes, and danced in an empty room, full hearts beating to a beating drum that called and beckoned and spurred us on.

We hugged and cried as dad closed the van door and Rich put the key in the ignition. We cried and clung to a life once was, our futures unfrozen by a push of motherly love that saw the promise in our eyes, alight with hope for heathered hills, purple clad and sprawling on. I turned and waved, they waved, two specs receding, left behind.

Mum and dad came to visit with a stuffed unicorn in an Asda bag. They cooed at my mountains and my sea. Mum put a shell in her pocket, a piece of Scotland for the mantel piece. Dad looked tired but mum said not mention it. They smiled and nodded in affirmation, this new future the right choice in their eyes, in our eyes. Rich's mum never came.

We did it. I did it. Built that life I'd always dreamed of, mostly for her, but also for me. She could be free and wild, have the sea for a home, the hills for a playground. A new place to call home. I built that life for that baby bouncing on my knee. I planted roses and lupins in the garden, we bought chickens, more babies came. Pockets full of shells, a shelf full of books. A life full rounded, well used, where winds yank my hair, and grains of sand on my shoes are worn like diamonds. We settled here, grew roots, a land of big skies and fishing boats, gala weeks, whiskey peat smells drifting on my way to fetch the milk. There're still the girls in puffa coats vaping and eating skittles, and I smile at them because, why not, they too just trying to build a life. Rich stares at me, a knowing in those sapphire eyes with splashes of gold, and I stare back.

Here is home, this place we settled in, where we settled for nothing less than the epiphany of perfection.

Jane Murton-Armer, originally from England, now lives in Caithness with her family. She began writing in 1996 and has had poems published in poetry magazines and poetry anthologies. She has just written the first draft a novel and is busy editing. Jane is currently studying a masters degree in Highlands & Islands Literature. Jane also enjoys reading, gardening and walks on the beach.

My Warning
Elizabeth Carey

When I am old I will choose when I wish to get up in the morning,
I will eat toast and marmalade in bed and not worry about the crumbs.
I will write to my heart's content about anything and everything that comes into my mind
and send it off to publishers who will reject it, and I won't worry.

When I am old I will do what I want, when I want and do nothing if that is what I choose.
I will eat dessert before the main course and enjoy every morsel.
I will indulge in having an afternoon gin and tonic with my neighbour and not be concerned
about what anybody thinks.

When I am old I will wear bright coloured clothes and floppy hats in the sunshine and if the weather permits swim in the sea.
I will sit under the umbrella in the garden, talk to the butterflies and the bees and take time
to stop and smell the roses.

When I am old I will still be first up on the dance floor and last off it.
I will play music loudly when I feel like it and sing out of tune.
I will keep the disco lights flashing as I dance around the living room
and I won't have a care in the world.

When I am old, I will still tend my garden, my vegetables, my flowers,
it may take me a bit longer, but I will take time and be careful and follow everyone's instructions - NOT!
Inwardly I will be careful as my old knees creak.

When I am old I won't see the sagging skin on my body
as I tiptoe from the bathroom with no clothes on.
Only the image of the young blithe spirit of 'thirty something'
in the bedroom mirror, I will just smile and embrace every wrinkle .

When I am old I will do housework when I feel like it, not as a day to day regime
I will enjoy watching the spider in his cobweb in the corner of the room,
I will acknowledge his life is precious too and he needs his home
I will not be quick to remove him.

When I am old I will be choosy with what groups to join.
I will be more careful about not becoming embroiled in the politics
and gossip, and I most certainly will not contribute to what
could become very difficult circumstances for all concerned.

When I am old I will look out to sea and wistfully recapture the memories
Of bygone days and be thankful for them.
I will shed buckets of tears at sad movies and not care
If people around me tell me to get a grip and 'shhhhh.'

When I am old I will take time to share words with others
To take pleasure in every syllable I write
as if it were a precious jewel to be cast wide upon
The vast ocean of like minded souls.

When I am old, I will challenge myself
To tackle topics I have never dreamt of
I will research happily not because I have to
I will allow my daydreams to become structured and meaningful.

In fact, when I am old, which, of course I will never admit too, I will enjoy every moment of every day, I will enjoy the feeling of the warmth of the sun on my skin, I will enjoy the seasons of the year, I will enjoy the fact that I have had a wonderful fulfilled life, with no regrets and I will shout that from the rooftops if I so desire and when *I* feel like it - *SO BEWARE*

.

Elizabeth Carey is currently featured in Issue 12 Season 8 No 96 of Dreich Magazine published by Jack Caradoc and Strathkelvin Writers' Group Anthology 'Sky Painting.' She corresponds regularly with two writers' groups in Queensland Australia and participates in Zoom sessions. She has performed at Tidelines Winter Warmer sessions in the Harbour Arts Centre Irvine. A member of the Federation of Writers Scotland she challenges herself to submit work on a monthly basis to destinations offering submission windows.

Cobwebs
Elizabeth Carey

Hearts hardened, heads phone gawking,
egotistical foolishness.
Nature wails, science shakes its fist,
consequences are apparent.
Wars, fires, droughts, is change too late?
How can we lure truth out from its
global sticky web of deceit?
Deniars, liars have become the norm.
Greed and power before need.
Truth, hidden by years of indifference,
dumbed down by apathy.
How can we restore direction?
How can we halt the self-destruct button?

Hold on to hope, reach for
that precious rainbow
on the horizon to
light, guide and direct.
Seek inner peace through
stillness in our chaotic world.
Focus hearts and minds
on positivity.
Harmony and love will truly follow.
Don't allow negative influences to
overtake resolve and snare us
into its web.

Dichotomy
Leigh Sosville

Pibrochs play on the misty moor
overwhelming you with the foustie scent of heather.
Scaling low like a stealthy serpent,
influencing your morose mood.
Trust yourself; what trust is there?
In the Highlands
vexed by the raucous cry of crows,
in despair.
Towering mountains and unending glens,
you yearn for what is yet to be.

Positivity.

Never give up,
endure like birch sap and sustain the tree through the seasons.
Greet each dawn with your head above water, like
a boundless bouncing buoyancy aid,
trusting yourself and the path that
ignites your exuberant mood.
Vivid landscapes, wild and free,
inspiring tales from history.
The clans unite.
You are content with what is.

Leigh Sosville is a poet and creative non-fiction writer with a passion for the arts and humanities. Her work spans a range of creative practices, through which she invites readers to delve into the connections between environment, myth, and well-being. Since relocating from Oxford, England, to Caithness in 2019, Sosville has been immersing herself in the rich history and unique bioregion of the Highlands. She is currently developing a collection of eco-poems that celebrate the crucial role of fungi in sustaining ecological balance and enhancing the health of diverse living organisms within our ecosystems.

A Cat Called Connie
S. Bee.

"I told you about this party weeks ago!' Holly said, as she sprayed on perfume.

Joe, Holly's car mechanic partner, who she lived with, looked puzzled. "Did you?"

"Yes, I did. I can't miss this party, Joe! It's really important for my future and my career."

Holly was a highly successful beauty vlogger, and had recently been invited to a glittering, glamorous, celebrity thronged party.

She was thrilled that the host, the regional head of a famous cosmetics brand, had included her as a guest!

This party is going to be fantastic for networking, she thought. She had to sparkle and schmooze, because she wanted to clinch a reality TV role... that's why it's so important to look my best!

All the familiar 'in crowd' faces would be there – pop singers, TV stars, models, soap actors and actresses, plus she hoped that the powerful TV producers and directors would be in attendance, too.

On a personal level, as a dedicated animal lover, Holly made sure that she chose make-up that had not been tested on animals in any way.

She was looking forward to meeting a well- known TV vet, Maggie Riley.

She and Joe enjoyed watching Maggie's documentary programme. It portrayed a host of pet problems and Maggie's patient and kind nature soothed pet owner's frazzled nerves.

Joe and Holly tuned in every week.

"So, I suppose I'm not invited to this party?" Joe's voice brought Holly back to the moment.

She shook her head. "No. I'm sorry, Joe. Look, we'll go somewhere nice together later. Maybe the cinema."

"I guess the party is for media types only, eh?" He smiled wryly.

"Well, the invites were pretty exclusive," she replied, as she focused on her final touches to her appearance. It was essential to get those accessories exactly right!

Joe hovered. "Shall I drive you there? Or phone for a taxi?"

"There's no need for either. It's within walking distance," she said, as she threw keys, mobile and her purse into a tiny sparkly handbag, scooped up her new bright pink satin jacket and crammed her feet into high heels. "Bye! Don't wait up!"

"Have a good time. Keep safe, and call me if you need me!" Joe called.

***

Holly's beauty vlog had thousands of followers.

It had started as a little hobby, yet over time, it had attracted more followers, especially when she'd begun to use all the social media platforms.

Her hard work and persistence paid off and she appeared across a wide range of national media. She was interviewed on podcasts – then she was offered her own beauty section in a monthly magazine.

Now cosmetics companies employed her to promote their products.

On her way to the party, in a city centre street, she spotted a thin black cat hurrying along the pavement.

Holly absolutely loved cats. Her parents had kept a cat as a family pet.

She'd grown up with soft purrs and waking up to a warm bundle of fur on her bed, plus there was lots of cuddles and affection!

In fact, Holly was hoping that she and Joe could adopt a moggy from an animal rescue shelter... she kept an eye on the fearful stray.

The poor puss was eager to get out people's way. It was probably hungry, she thought. It was out alone, on a dark, cold night.. her heart melted.

Oh how sad! Hmm, she thought. I have an idea...

***

At the party, Holly spotted Sarah, who was the CEO of an animal rescue charity. They'd already met, as they'd previously been part of a panel for a radio phone- in show.

She mentioned the ebony kitty to Sarah. "Well, you've come to the right person, Holly. I can help you tonight. Let me make a phone call."

Holly beamed. "Great!"

While Sarah fished out her mobile, Holly looked around the chatty throng.

To her dismay, she couldn't see Maggie Riley.

Well, maybe a star studded champagne party wouldn't really appeal to the sensible, down to earth vet, she reasoned.

"There's a vacant pen at a local animal shelter," Sarah said. "Let's go out and find this cat."

Holly hesitated. "What - right now?"

She'd assumed that Sarah, being the big boss, would allocate the task to someone else.

Of course, Holly wanted to rescue the puss – but equally, she didn't want to miss her chance to work the room. There was a precious reality TV role at risk!

"It'd be good to take action straight away," Sarah explained. "I keep a spare cat carrier in my car and I have a stock of cat food in easy to open sachets, bottles of tap water and feeding bowls."

Holly smiled. "Oh, that's good to hear."

"We can put food and drink in the bowls and place these inside the carrier. The smell will tempt the kitty inside. When we've dropped the cat off, we can return to the party," Sarah went on.

Holly nodded. They explained the situation quickly to the host and headed out.

After they'd filled the bowls with cat food and water, Sarah carefully scooped up her cat carrier and the pair cautiously approached the street where Holly had spotted the kitty.

But Holly's heart sank - there was no sign of the cat.

Then Sarah touched Holly's arm "Look - down there!"

Holly peered down a back alley, where the feline's green eyes shone on the moonlight.

Cautious and wary, the duo approached slowly, not wanting to scare the animal.

To Holly's surprise, the stray didn't race away - it was as if the puss sensed they were here to help.

Sarah stopped and opened the door of the cat carrier.

"We step back now," she whispered.

They watched in the dim shadows, as the hesitant kitty rose to its feet. It sniffed and padded closer, until it ambled into the cat carrier.

Sarah quickly closed the door and secured the catch.

"There! All done!" she beamed.

As they headed towards Sarah's car, Holly happened to glance up at the street name. This Victorian back alley was called 'Constance Place.'

They drove to the animal shelter, where the vet on duty gave the stray flea and worm treatment. Holly and Sarah discovered that the cat was female.

Then she was placed in a warm pen, with a cosy bed. There was a litter tray, soft blankets, pet toys, plus bowls of food and water.

"After the stray has got used to human company, we can put her up for adoption," Sarah outlined.

"I'd love to offer her a home," Holly asked. "But I'd need to discuss with Joe first."

"I really hope he says yes. We won't need to upload this new cat's details onto this branch's website if you adopt her. All of our branches have an adoption section on their websites, where people can view the pets who need a home."

Holly nodded. She'd often browsed the 'Adopt a cat' section herself...

***

Twenty minutes later, Holly bid Sarah a fond farewell. Sarah was calling it a night - she'd only gone to the party to show her face.

Right, Holly thought. Let's get back to mingling and mixing!

Yet she stopped. Tonight's experience had changed things. Holly unexpectedly found herself making her way home.

After rescuing a starving cold cat, in desperate need of TLC, ingratiating herself with 'important' media people somehow didn't seem such a high priority.

There was nothing wrong with ambition, but now she realised there were more important things in life than being 'in with in crowd.'

***

A few nights later, Holly and Joe were snuggled up on the sofa as they watched telly. Holly's favourite programme with vet Maggie Riley was about to begin.

There were loads of stray cats out there, she thought.

Well, it was time to think about how she could raise income for Sarah's charity.

She could get in touch with Maggie and maybe she'd like to team up with Holly for a new pet themed vlogging project... it was all about taking positive action!

This reminded her - she turned to Joe.

"How would you feel about adopting a cat?" she asked.

Joe smiled. "I'd love to."

Holly's spirit warmed. "That's settled then. Sarah and I rescued a lovely black cat the other evening. She's at the rescue shelter and she's looking for a new home. She needs a name, though."

"I'll leave that to you," he said.

Holly reflected... where had she and Sarah found the stray? At Constance Place.

"How about the name Connie?"

He considered. "Hmm. A cat called Connie? That sounds good."

She grinned. "It does, doesn't it?"

S. Bee. is a fifty- something, happily married and she lives in a small town in West Yorkshire.

She has had several short stories published in women's magazines, Plus, she has had quite a few letters and rhyming poems published in magazines, too.

The Luckiest Boy in the World
Steve Wade

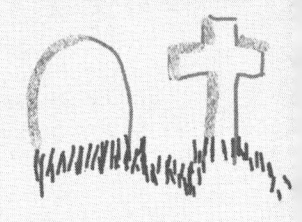

He was smiling at me now over the tops of the headstones that separated us. "How's the man?" he said through cupped hands encircling his mouth.

I can't stomach intrusive friendliness and shot him a half-hearted wave.

I'd been aware of this guy watching me since I entered the cemetery. I was there to check up on Danny, my little buddy, to tell him I'd been thinking about him everyday since my last visit at Christmas. The thoughts of him all alone, confused and frightened during the long winter nights I'd tried to banish by numbing myself with enough beer to keep me permanently ill crippled me with shame. I'd used the bad weather as an excuse to stay away. But this was the first glorious day that springtime. I could sense it in the air the moment I opened the bedroom window that morning. I could almost smell the sweetness pouring from the soft breaths of songbirds. They seemed to have smiles inserted into their singing. I called in sick to the office, had a late breakfast, took the cover off my Kawasaki Vulcan in the shed, tanked her up and headed out of the city for the lonely country roads that led to the graveyard.

Striking up a conversation with the only other person in the cemetery was distorting my plan. I began to shove off.

"Hey Jonathan," he called after me.

Shit. This guy was someone from the job was my first thought, or one of the hundreds of faces from another company, maybe, who work in the same building. Someone I'd been introduced to and had forgotten. I turned back to face him. He was coming at me with his arm already outstretched to shake my hand.

"Do you remember me?" he said, clamping my hand in both his hands and working my arm like an old-fashioned water-pump.

There was nothing memorable about him. He looked like every other guy and nobody. I didn't make it clear whether I remembered him or not. I just nodded. "My grandfather died this day ten years ago," I lied. "I take a day off to come out here - a kind of ritual for me now. How about you?"

He released my hand and squinted at the writing and photo on the white-marble headstone in front of us. I protested that, no, that wasn't his grave. I told him that he was buried at the far end. I swung my arm in the direction of the tall pine trees I climb into when there's no one else about. Gives me an altogether different overview looking down on the tidy rows of headstones, and beyond, outside the cemetery entrance, my silver and black bike gleaming and sparkling in the sunshine. Waiting for me, and for Danny, too.

"Harry," he said, offering me his damp hand again, the smile frozen on his face. "Harry Kinahan."

"Harry," I said. "I don't believe it. Harry." The last memory I located of Harry he was a fat teenager protecting his little sister, Nicolette, from my adolescent interest. "I'd never have … How the hell did you recognise me?"

He'd seen my name and picture in the paper. He'd followed the court-case. He was sorry, he said, he truly was, for all the parties concerned.

I could feel myself welling up but fought it. The bottomless reserve-tanks no longer surprised me. I went over the details with him and answered most of his questions.

One thing that puzzled him though was why I'd let it go to court, why I hadn't just accepted culpability from the start, and avoided all that hassle and heartache. Given my clean record, the judge might have shown me some leeway, and not made an example of me by putting me away for – "How long was it?" he wanted to know.

I'd explained myself too often to others. Only if you're in such a situation could you understand that denial, even when you know you're guilty, is a way of destabilising the truth, of shucking off responsibility.

I told Harry that I really didn't want to go into it. Things were still way too raw. I flicked my eyes at Danny's photo-image inset into the headstone. A short high-pitched note I was unable to stifle leaked from my throat. Two years on and it affected me yet.

"He was a smashing looking boy," Harry said. He shook his head and clucked his tongue a few times.

Why did people always comment on Danny's appearance? Did it make it worse that he hadn't resembled Quasimodo, or been an insignificant street kid whose parents sent out to beg on the streets? Probably.

In the picture Danny's creased eyes suggested he'd been laughing when the photo was taken. This was the only image I had of him. Almost three weeks had ticked by when I came out from a coma, a coma from which the doctors informed me I should never have emerged. As soon as I learned that I'd been responsible for ending the life of a seven-year-old kid, a kid whose lifeless body was already buried beneath the earth, I was in full agreement with the doctors – I should never have woken up; should never have been allowed to wake up.

Straight off they put me on suicide watch. Luckily, for me, the pain from the injuries I'd sustained in the accident was so great they had me on heavy medication for most of the time. I either slept, or my senses were too clogged and groggy to contemplate the full import of killing a child.

Using his nascent psychology, I guessed, Harry asked me if I was a family man myself. He was changing the subject, veering me away from the horror.

I shook my head.

"A girlfriend then?"

"Nope," I said, which, I could see, threw him by dismissing before he'd asked it, the real question he'd been leading up to: How about my own kids?

I didn't deserve to have kids. I'd thought about it a lot. Going on living was betrayal enough to Danny, the laughing boy, whose laughter I had ended. What right had I to foster counterfeit laughter from genes that had cheated destiny? Besides, I'd come to regard Danny as the son I'd never have - that, and a kind of kid brother, too.

"It's just me and the Vulcan," I said to Harry. I chucked my chin in the direction of the cemetery entrance.

This seemed to relieve his momentary awkwardness. He became animated talking about bikes, beads of sweat slipping down his forehead, as he strained for the relevant terminology, but I could see through his forced enthusiasm. Harry hadn't a notion about motorbikes.

About to crank-up and speed off into the story of the hours I'd spent there in the beginning, seated in the earth before Danny's grave, I stopped myself. No one got it - except Danny. He understood. At first I figured that perhaps the accident had loosened a few bolts inside me, jolted some connections out of place, but it seemed there was no other way of dealing with what happened. I spoke to Danny's picture, never for an instant while we talked doubting that he could hear me – the initial doubts came during the sleepless nights.

Back at his graveside, Danny's boyhood energy and inquisitiveness banished every doubt. I told Danny everything, brought him right back to when I was his age. He got to meet my buddies and do all the stuff we did. We went bird-nesting among the bramble-bushes. We larked about in the fields, worrying farmer O'Reilly's cattle until they lined up to stampede, which sent us yipping and yapping like coyotes and pelting for the cover of the trees.

Unlike the rest of us, my buddies and me, Danny didn't stretch overnight out of his clothes, nor did he grow stronger and faster. With every visit to his graveside, I brought Danny on new and exciting adventures. I watched out for him. If one of the gang shouted 'Skinheads," I grasped Danny's hand and ran with him to freedom, his tiny legs pounding faster than they should have over the sun-hardened earth, and his frightened and excited laugh wobbling with the movement.

Like a herd of wild mustang, the years galloped by. I was on my third bike, the Vulcan, and Danny remained the same, the luckiest boy in the world, the boy who remained a boy forever.

Of course, it was inevitable that I wouldn't always be there to look out for Danny. That I was the one he had to be guarded against became the greatest irony.

Mid-June, a few days shy of my twenty-seventh birthday. I'd taken my new bike out for its first real run, up over the mountains and into the Lake District. There I parked the Vulcan and sat down with my back supported against the bole of an old sycamore. While I sucked in the crumbling evening, I made up a rollie, a strong one, and cracked open a few lagers.

When it got dark, I cranked up the bike's engine, revved her up, and let her sit for a bit before heading off. On the way down the mountains, I kept my speed down and cruised safely for home. Back in the city my head wasn't working too well and my eyes felt filled with grit. The last thing I remember from that day was taking a right turn into my parents' street to our house, and wondering how come there was a new bridge I'd never noticed.

Going over the bridge, I stood up out of the saddle to check out the river below, or whatever it was. Sometimes I imagine I remember Danny's petrified face as he pedalled maniacally to make it across my path. But I'm sure it's just induced memory from what I've learned about that awful day.

Convincing Danny at his graveside that the Vulcan had been completely over-hauled and was one hundred per cent safe was hard. More difficult still was persuading him to overcome his justifiable fear at my insistence that the only way to get over a trauma was to confront its cause. That's what I did.

Back to Harry: I was getting a bit edgy with his presence. I made a point at looking at my watch - nearly time for Danny and me to head off to McDonald's in the local town. And I hadn't even said 'Hello' to the boy yet.

Harry seemed to catch my not-so-subtle hint. He said he was sorry for keeping me but before he let me go, there was someone he'd like me to say 'Hello' to. It would only take a minute or so.

In my head I told Danny to *Hang in there, kiddo*, and promised him I'd be back in a second. I followed Harry in silence to the side of the cemetery. Wearing a smile that wasn't a smile, he rounded a row of uniformed-sized headstones and stopped before a wooden crucifix, looked at me where I stood behind the grave and nodded down on the cross.

I stepped up next to Harry and read the simple inscription: Nicolette Godwin R.I.P.

"Just before Christmas," he said. "She'd been married just two months. An aneurysm. Her husband found her at the bottom of the stairs." Harry went on to tell me that they pulled the plug on his sister after four weeks. She'd morphed into a skeleton. The worst part of it was she'd been carrying a baby. Nicolette had been so looking forward to motherhood, he explained.

Something beat a steady tattoo behind my eyes, and in my chest I felt a rising flood of boundless joy. As soon as Danny and I got back from lunch, I'd get reacquainted with the only girl who ever noticed me. She and Danny would hit it off straight away. How could she resist Danny?

Never again would I wake up in the night, shivering though lathered in sweat at the thought of Danny cold, alone and lonely in the country graveyard. Nicolette was there to watch over him now.

Steve Wade's short story collection, 'In Fields of Butterfly Flames and Other Stories' was published in 2020. His award-winning short fiction has been widely published and anthologised. He has had stories shortlisted for the Francis McManus Short Story Competition and for the Hennessy Award. His stories have appeared in over seventy print publications. He has won First Prize in the Delvin Garradrimna Short Story Competition on four occasions. Winner of the Short Story category in the Write by the Sea writing competition 2019. Joint First Prize Winner in the John McGivering Prize 2022. He was a prize nominee for the PEN/O'Henry Award, and a prize nominee for the Pushcart Prize.

Near Catastrophe
Brenda Lawrence

Cool cat, perilous quest

Across the shelf where vases rest

Teasing whiskers test the gaps

As velvet paws avoid mishaps

Sylph-like movements spring to ground

Tantamount there be no sound

Rubbing, loving slippered feet

Of course you can jump up on seat

Purr you may your goal achieved

Happy owner, cat relieved

Enjoyment sleeping on warm knee

      So far, so near catastrophe!

Born in the south of England, Brenda relocated with her teenage family to Scotland in the early 1970s. Since then, she has spent most of her working life as a crofter until reluctantly having to retire due to ill-health and frailty. Formerly residing in Caithness, she has recently moved south to be closer to family. An enthusiastic writer, she now lives with her partner near Inverness.

Thanks a Bunch
Brenda Lawrence

'Morning Harry,' called Madge, pulling on her overalls in the polytunnel. 'See there's been another delivery, no peace for the wicked, eh?' she sighed, running her eyes over the trolley load of plants. With the hose training behind her, she headed for the far end of the tunnel.

'Give the vine a drink while you're at it,' reminded Harry, up to his elbows in potting compost.

Madge crossed to the ancient plant and gave the roots a thorough soaking. She had a soft spot for the old vine which despite its gnarled appearance had produced an abundance of fruit over the years and this season was no exception.

'Looks like you could do with another pair of hands,' called the garden centre manager, poking his head in the tunnel. He hadn't told Harry and Madge the name of their new trainee but whoever it was they'd certainly made an impression on him.

'Who is it? Is it someone local?' they asked expectantly.

The manager laughed. 'Sort of,' he said, glancing sideways.

When Madge saw him standing there she almost fainted on the spot.

'Do you remember…?'

'Murphy,' interrupted Madge and Harry in unison, 'Murphy Maguire, of course we remember,' they groaned, exchanging worried looks.

'Hello Harry, hello Mrs M,' he said politely, wearing the familiar boyish grin they'd come to know and dread. 'You haven't changed one bit. I've been wanting to come back and see you for years.'

'C'mon, let's get you kitted out,' intervened the manager, sensing an air of unease. Taking hold of Murphy's arm, he shepherded him off, tossing a reassuring grin over his shoulder.

Madge turned to Harry, her heart hammering wildly. Murphy Maguire without exaggeration, was a name to strike fear and trepidation into the heart of many a grown adult. True he'd grown up into a handsome young chap but then he'd always been a good-looking little boy. When the family moved to the other side of town and he began attending a different school you could hear the sighs of relief for miles around. Murphy was her grandson Jamie's best pal and during their friendship, she learned a thing or two about his upbringing. He lived alone with his divorced mother and as far as Madge could gather, was never allowed to be a child. At home he had to be an angel so when out and about or visiting other people's places, he turned into a little horror. And for some reason, he seemed to like spending time with Harry and Madge better than anywhere else.

Having got her breath back, Madge stripped the protective layer from around the trolley and began dealing with the assortment of plants. Always one step ahead, she'd everything to hand; water-filled containers for fresh flowers, moist trays for the seasonal pot plants, overhead hooks for a few hanging baskets and a dry sunny corner for the cacti collection. Satisfied with her efforts, she wiped her hands on her overalls and turned her attention to the specialised orchids positioning each one carefully in their allocated spot on the benches.

'A place for everything and everything in its place,' Harry beamed, making room for a tray of miniature succulents. 'Don't know about you Madge but I'm starting to get a bit peckish.' Delving into his rucksack, he pulled out his mid-morning snack.

'See the grapevine's survived,' coughed Murphy embarrassingly, startling the unsuspecting pair.

'The grapevine,' Madge gasped, reliving the horror of the day when she found him straddling the benches stripping the vine of the ripening grapes and catapulting them the length of the polytunnel.

'They're sour,' he'd spluttered fearfully, hastily dropping a half-eaten bunch, his hands shaking as he'd tried to wipe the telltale stains from around his mouth and chin. Madge had looked on with bated breath as he'd swung himself off the bench and landing with a thump had kept a wide berth. Well you would, wouldn't you!

'What's wrong Madge?' Harry asked, interrupting her thoughts. 'Is there something troubling you?'

'Don't leave Murphy on his own in the polytunnel, do you hear?' she hissed determinedly, nodding towards the heavily laden vine. 'I'm off to get him something to eat, the lad's starving.'

'Nothing new there then,' said Harry, his face breaking out in a broad grin, 'here take this loose change,' he said, scrounging about in his overall pocket. 'Get a packet of those chocolate digestives while you're at it, they're his favourites remember?'

Madge recalled how Murphy used to empty their lunchboxes when he came to visit. She wouldn't have minded him having an apple or banana but he'd be straight into the sandwiches and when they were gone he'd start on the snack bars and crisps. She could never understand why a lad with such a ravenous appetite could be so skinny but then he was always on the go. He couldn't stay still for a minute!

Whatever Madge thought of Murphy, time had not erased from her mind the image of that little boy being led away by his father, tears streaming down his face. And the worst of it was, she knew it was all her fault. 'It's because of that plant isn't it?' he'd wailed, his face red and crumpled. 'I'm sorry Mrs M, didn't mean it no harm.'

After the incident in the polytunnel Madge had held his trembling hands in hers, trying to calm him. She'd never seen a child in such a state before. It was then that it all came out and there was no stopping him. How his mother had no time for him and kept him short of food but that wasn't the worst of it. His greatest fear was that Madge would tell her and he knew what would be in store for him. She was the one person in the world he should have been able to trust, to feel safe with, yet he seemed terrified of her.

All it had taken was one phone-call.

'We've never met Mr Maguire, but it's about your son, Murphy…'

Madge would never forget the churning feeling in the pit of her stomach after learning of the lad's miserable existence behind closed doors. Nor would she forget the agony of the decision she knew she'd had to make. And here he was back to haunt her. Did he really think it was because of the grapevine that his father had come to take him away? Had he thought all these years that she'd called his father out of spite?

Madge returned carrying a tray of steaming mugs, a packet of biscuits sticking out of her overall pocket. Murphy grinned up at her, that same cheeky lop-sided grin she knew of old.

'Coffee?' she asked, mustering up a smile.

'Coffee would be great and chocolate digestives too! Aw, thanks a bunch Mrs M this all reminds me of when I was a kid,' he said, wolfing down the last of Harry's cheese and pickle sandwiches. 'If it hadn't been for you and my dad, I wouldn't have had a childhood.'

With his eyes shining a little too brightly, he reached out to Madge and put his arm around her shoulders and that's when she knew. It wasn't revenge that had brought Murphy back into her life but something more positive. It was his undying gratitude.

Ornithologising
Greg Michaelson

They say we're naught but twitchers. They say we're naught but nerds.
They say we don't have time to talk; we don't have time for words.
Our only friends are feathery; our only friends are birds.
When we all go an ornithologising.

There are great tits, blue tits, ravens, crows and owls.
There are blackbirds, jackdaws, sparrows, larks and gulls.
There are kestrels, eagles, kites and water fowl.
When we all go an ornithologising.

I spend all day beside a lathe, assembling cuckoo clocks.
The lass that carves the wooden birds, likes knitting stripy socks.
She says one day we'll build a nest and raise our own wee flock.
And we'll all go an ornithologising.

There are coots and moorhens, herons, cranes and storks.
There are magpies, goldfinch, hen harriers and hawks.
There are spoonbills, osprey, greylag geese and auks.
When we all go an ornithologising.

We'll ramble by the Figgate Burn, binoculars in hand.
We'll ramble down Cockenzie way, along the golden sand.
We'll ramble up on Blackford Hill, our bonnie birding band,
When we all go an ornithologising.

There are pigeons, partridge, ptarmigan and wrens.
There are peacock, robins, cormorants and hens.
There are doves and curlew, our soaring squawking friends,
When we all go an ornithologising.

(For Anna.)

Greg Michaelson is an Edinburgh based writer, whose short stories have been published for over 20 years. His post apocalyptic novel The Wave Singer (Argyll, 2008), set on the dry sea bed of the Moray Firth, was shortlisted for a Scottish Arts Council/Scottish Mortgage Investment Trust First Book award. Subsequently, he was granted a SAC Writer's Bursary. During lockdown, he and Ruth Aylett wrote the Science Fiction/Fantasy cross over Equinox (Stairwell, 2023), about how attempts to extract green energy under Rannoch moor break the multiverse. Greg likes to write about how things aren't and how they might be.

The End of Helen L.'s Dream
Robert Tateson

Helen L. was searching for something, something she thought she had lost. That morning was her eighty seventh birthday and she had lost the end of her dream.

She had been woken suddenly by her ginger cat, Leo. He had jumped on her head. Now she was trying to remember the part of the dream she never had, it was neither a pleasant nor an unpleasant dream. She remembered the beginning, it was a walk in the zoo. Now that she was awake, she wished she knew how the walk ended.

She found her glasses, fed Leo, had a cup of tea, put on her tweed hat and coat, checked that her bus pass was in her handbag and caught the No 31 to Edinburgh Zoo.

Helen L. stopped in front of a cage holding a lion.

If I put my head through the bars, will the lion pounce on it and wake me up, the way Leo did? Perhaps life is nothing but a waking dream.

A stinging flurry of hail rattled in off the Firth of Forth.

No, this is real. My dream was a dream.

She explored the Reptile House. A solitary lizard turned its head, keeping eye contact with her as she crab-walked past. Part of its tail was missing.

Has it eaten its own tail? Is it growing a new tail from the nutrition of the old? Was my dream a circle with no end and no beginning?

She turned to the side of the building and left by a different door.

Outside, the hail had stopped and she followed the signposts saying 'The Australian Paddock'. Before navigators thought they had discovered Australia, everyone in Edinburgh knew that all swans were white. Helen L. watched the black swans sailing before the breeze on the silver lake.

I have never had a nightmare. The end of my dream might have been a nightmare, but I doubt it.

Some kangaroos hopped over the grass. One had a joey in its pouch.

I wonder if the joey has a pouch too. Does the joey have a joey-joey in its pouch, and that one a joey-joey-joey and so on?

A zoo keeper hummed by on an electric buggy pulling a trailer of hay.

That buggy doesn't have a little buggy inside to make it go. It just has batteries and a motor.

She drifted across to the Aquarium. A teacher was pointing out tropical fish to excited pupils. Helen L. stood quietly above a pool of brown trout and fished for them with her eyes.

I caught many of those when I was younger. Lost some too. What does that remind me of? No man can lose that which he never had.

"That's it!"

Helen L. startled the children. They turned and gawped at her, some giggled.

"It's time to go home and feed the cat."

The teacher shook her head, the way one does with a harmless, batty old woman.

When Helen L. returned to her garden the full moon had risen.

"Puss, puss, puss! Leo! Puss, puss puss! Fish for tea! Fish, fish, fish! Leeeeeeo!"

A dark shape unfolded from the corner and strutted across the moonlit grass.

"Here Leo!"

But that's not Leo. It's only his shadow.

She glanced up. Leo was stalking the moon on top of the wall.

I thought I saw Leo but what I saw was everything that wasn't Leo.

Helen L. made herself a cup of tea, sat in her old armchair and waited for Leo to jump onto her lap.

"The end of my dream was never there, Leo."

The cat purred.

"The end of my dream was nothing. Death is nothing. The shadow of nothing is everything. Isn't that wonderful."

Robert Tateson was born in Sheffield, and studied genetics at Edinburgh University. After working as a research scientist, he backtracked to a steel rolling mill. Eventually he was washed up on the shores of Orkney where he supported himself and his family as a crofter and milkman before surrendering to fate and becoming the maths/science teacher on the small island of Stronsay. He has now retired with his cat to Kinlochbervie where he enjoys growing vegetables and writing short stories. He has had some success being published once in Hooded and twice in the Plaza Prizes.

Printed in Great Britain
by Amazon